BLOOD PACT

The Fourth in the
Cycle of the Aphotic World

THE APHOTIC SERIES

Bad Blood
Out For Blood
Blood Loss
Blood Pact
Blood Relations
Flesh and Blood

BLOOD PACT

Tobin Elliott

This one is about finding your family. So this one goes out to my two brothers, Ryan and Dale. You're both better men than I'll ever hope to be, but you make me want to be better. And that's what brothers do. They lift you up. Oh, and you both make me laugh hard enough to puke. So, there's that, too.

Acknowledgements

You'll find many of the same people here as in every acknowledgement page I do. To the Hickeys and the Longs. To my son and my son-in-law, and to my daughter and daughter-in-law, and of course, to my wife. You are the ones who drive me crazy, and you're the ones who keep me sane. You are my family.

To Jennifer Dinsmore, who gasps in all the right places, gets grossed out in all the right places, and gives me shit in all the right places, all while applying her prodigious editing skills that make me look better than I am. And, at no point up to now has she questioned my sanity.

A special call out to Lori (you know who you are). You gave me two gifts. The first was to force me out of my shyness in grade eleven. The second was to tell me about a certain accident involving a boat and a coffin…and, when I said I'd never heard of it, exclaim, "How could you have lived here for that many years and not know it?" See? Some do question my sanity.

"We few. We happy few. We band of brothers."

— William Shakespeare

PROLOGUE

1953

CHLOE STOOD AT the front door to Will's home. His birthday party was coming to a critical moment, and Chloe was there to ensure it went the right way. The way she needed it to go.

But she would be Glory.

She looked down the street to the boy standing under a store awning, in the shade. Red. Her constant companion. Her brother.

She gave him a look. He nodded once, then held up two fingers. She knew what that meant.

You saved me. Twice.

That brought a flood of memories.

◆ ◆ ◆

1911

THE SUMMER MOON hung low, its reflection doubled in the lake. The night was calm, with barely a breeze to ripple the water. Far off, on the other side of Lake Kwanashishing, Chloe spied the flickering campfires and caught the indistinct voices of men over the lapping waters.

Closer, she heard the night creatures crawling, walking, slithering, or flying through the forest. She'd had to stand very still for a very long time before they came back out from hiding at her passing, and found the courage to start up their tasks and night songs again.

Chloe was alone.

She didn't enjoy being alone, but it was often preferable to dealing with others. At least when she was alone, she could let her thoughts crawl or walk or slither or fly wherever they wanted to go.

Tonight, her thoughts led her here, to this shore.

Lake Kwanashishing was shaped like an hourglass, if that hourglass had been drawn by a quivering hand. A wide, deep bowl at both the northern end, where the town of New Hope sat, and the same at the southern end, where the residents of Carry's Cove resided. In between, the lake narrowed, got shallower, and kept much of its treachery hidden.

Chloe stood toward the southern end, just before the lake widened back out before ending at Carry's Cove. She gazed upon the expanse of water, and watched the meagre lights of the cove.

But she could not go there.

She stood only a few feet from the boundary. The boundary that marked where her kind were allowed to be, and where they were not.

A large, dry branch, downed by some bothersome wind, lay just off to the side. She approached it, let her hand gently touch the rough surface. *What was once a living thing is no longer.* Yet, aside from the location of the branch, it didn't appear dead. *Appearing alive, but not.*

Her hand tightened on the wood, her wrist twisted, and she cracked off a foot-long section.

She sidearmed it into the lake, the force of her swing taking the branch well out to the middle of the narrows before it hit the water.

She watched it then, bobbing as the current pushed it southward into the widened bowl of the lake, pushing it toward the town she could only see from a distance.

Because of the werewolves, she thought.

She snapped off another twig, and spun it into the water.

Chloe was a member of a Clutch, a group of men and women with the same unique abilities and hungers as her. At one time, before Chloe was born — so the details were somewhat foggy because the older Clutch members were incredibly reluctant to even think about it, let alone discuss it — her Clutch held dominion over the werewolves, stupid, bestial creatures that they were.

The werewolves, though powerful and numerous with their packs, could never overcome those of the Clutch.

Until they found the Book. Or the Book found them.

The Book was a legendary, mythical tome. She had heard rumours of a strange man in New England who was incorporating It into his fiction, but had, so far, had no luck in getting it published. Would that he never did, as his life would be far easier that way.

She broke off another, thicker section of branch. Hefted its weight. Threw it. It splashed satisfyingly before joining in the southward journey of its severed companions.

Your mind wanders, Chloe.

Regardless. In the very early 1800s, roughly thirty-five years after the uppity Americans to the south had announced their independence, and not quite six decades before this country did the same, the damnable wolves somehow gained access to the Book and were able to stake out a small boundary of about roughly two hundred square miles. In the centre was a bowl-shaped clearing that, fifty years later, would fall within the city limits of the town of Vilni.

Since then — about a hundred years now — this was the only area Chloe's Clutch could travel. Two hundred square miles was not a lot for a race that counted on being nomadic for their survival.

Over the time they had been locked within that boundary, they had probed and tested virtually every inch.

In that time, they had discovered three things.

First, in trying to discover weak spots, any Clutch member's first attempt at crossing the border resulted in them disappearing, then instantly reappearing at the exact centre of their two hundred square mile area, in the main street of Vilni.

Second, if the Clutch member was mad enough, or stupid enough, to make a second attempt, they simply disappeared. To where, no one knew, and no one cared to speculate. Nowhere good, to be sure.

Finally, they had determined, through their probing and testing, that there were no weak spots in the boundary.

Chloe reached down and picked up the rest of the branch. The remaining length still stood well above her head, maybe eight feet in length. She angled it back down and divided off a smaller section, the branch thicker than her wrist now.

Her throw arced it toward the water. Her sharp eyes watched the splash. Followed it as the stream took it.

Chloe knew that, over the years, many attempts had been made to bring the wolves into the boundaried area to open discussions with them. However, their attempts had always been rebuffed.

The wolves, despite using the Book to create the boundary, and knowing it affected only the Clutch members and no one else, still expressed reluctance to cross it, presumably fearing they might not get back out again due to coercion, death, or some form of trickery.

And their leader, Valda, had proven herself reluctant to bargain with those who had controlled them for so long.

Instead, they offered the Clutch their own challenge: meet the pack leader on their own soil, and arrangements would be discussed.

Or, put another way, find some method of escaping our trap, and we'll talk about allowing you to escape our trap.

A hopeless paradox.

Yes, their pack leader, this Valda, had proven herself to be a first-order bitch.

Chloe looked out on the water that flowed so easily past the artificial boundary, and she broke off another piece. She sent it spinning through the air, tracking where it landed, sending the smooth surface into chaotic disarray. But only for the moment. The water always found a way back.

From what Chloe had pieced together over the years, when the boundary was imposed the Clutch had been thrown into chaotic disarray as well. Used to roaming through nature's mansion to feed, they realized very quickly they were now trapped in a small closet. Since that time, it had taken a lot of work, but the Clutch had gone through a lot of change, including two different Firsts, and ultimately, they had learned to be careful. When their current First, Ileen, took over the Clutch, she enforced new rules, such as ensuring their numbers stayed low and feeding only as needed.

It was a painful change, but a necessary one.

And it had worked.

While they continued to be trapped in an area with several communities, it spoke to their success that these communities remained ones with no locks on the doors.

They had taken care to be discreet, to allow the communities they shared space with to feel safe.

After all, why lock something that would never be taken advantage of?

Chloe took the remaining length of branch and snapped it in two. She threw one of the pieces, easily tracking it through the night sky as it sailed effortlessly through the invisible barrier before falling into the water, well on the other side.

And the beginning of a thought whispered at the back of her mind.

She looked down at her hand, holding the last section of branch.

Stepping carefully out of the forest, onto the rocky shore, coming very close to the damnable border, she bent down. Placed the branch in the water. Pushed it out toward the centre of the narrows.

Her mind ticked over various thoughts as she watched it drift out, then angle toward the south. Toward freedom.

She kept coming back around to one thought.

Why lock something that would never be taken advantage of?

And then, *Why indeed?*

Chloe smiled as she turned away from the boundary and made her way back home to her Clutch.

PART ONE
LAUNCH

"I will not let you go into the unknown alone."

DRACULA
BRAM STOKER

Chapter One

1912

"THERE YOU GO, darlin'," the waitress said, setting a bowl of cream-laden oatmeal down in front of Chloe. The thin, raw-boned woman then pulled a tall glass of milk from the tray and set it beside the oatmeal. "That'll stick to your ribs," she said, smiling.

Chloe looked up at the woman, saw the frown lines around the mouth despite the put-on-for-the-customer smile. *She's twenty-four, but looks forty-four*, she thought.

Then, with a slight sense of wonder and satisfaction, she thought, *I'll never look that old.* "Thank you," Chloe said, giving the waitress her best little-girl smile. After the woman padded off to help a group of boisterous loggers, Chloe looked out the window of the restaurant.

The late November clouds hung low and heavy, seeming to press on the water of Lake Kwanashishing. She'd chosen today to do this because of the cloud cover, but it might turn against her.

There was another reason as well. Today was November 12 in, as they said, the year of our Lord, 1912. Today was the last day the *Mayflower* would make a run on Lake Kwanashishing.

Might snow tonight. That probably wouldn't help with what she needed to do.

Ah well, there was nothing to be done about it now. With

the exception of bending Captain Hudson to her will, everything else had been set in motion.

She saw no difficulty in bending Hudson to her will.

As she waited for her boat to come in, she took this rare daylight moment to observe. Through the windows of the diner and, indeed, within the diner itself, she watched those who she shared this land with go about their strangely fascinating, yet fruitless tasks. They went here and there, pushed on by their endless errands. They purchased items, or sold them, or traded them. They pushed foul-smelling substances, like the warming milk and the slowly congealing oatmeal in front of her, down their throats, though the benefit was transitory at best. And yet, they laughed. They seemed content, even happy with their lot, with their short lives and constant scrabbling for survival.

She would never understand how these creatures could find any sort of solace or contentment with the meaningless existence they had been shackled to. Not when there was so much more time, so much more power there.

As she stared at the inadequate meal that had been set at her table, she allowed herself a moment of smugness, of superiority to these fools who surrounded her.

Yet, inside, the constant, unwavering gnaw of the Eternal Hunger ate at her, demanding its price for keeping her not quite alive, but not yet dead.

Chapter Two

I T TOOK ANOTHER two hours—Chloe hadn't anticipated that long of a wait—before the long, squat, box-shaped *Mayflower* docked and Captain Hudson and his crew made her fast to the dock.

Chloe left enough change to cover the oatmeal, the milk, and the two subsequent teas that the waitress had dutifully brought and, with less and less joviality, dutifully taken away again, untouched. Chloe also left a generous tip.

She rose, pulled on the unnecessary coat, and trudged out of the diner, across the road, then down the hill to where the *Mayflower* was docked. Along the way, she squinted against the cloud cover—dull grey, yet still unbelievably bright to her sensitive eyes—then down to the ground at her feet. No shadow.

Having not been out during daylight in decades, she was unsure if it was just her, or the diffuse light that left no shadow. Looking at the other people, she saw strange, darkened areas on the ground where their bodies blocked some of the light. Such a bizarre phenomenon.

She would have to be careful of that.

For now, however, there was nothing to be done for it. She set her sights on the squat, boxy boat ahead of her, and continued on her path.

She knew exactly who Captain Hudson was, but still she played the role of the somewhat confused and fearful child to the hilt, asking first one deckhand, then a second, to direct her to the man.

When the second deckhand, a scrawny boy not yet old enough to grow more than a whisper of shade under his nose and chin, presented her to Captain Hudson, she waited for him to remove the smouldering pipe from his mouth and look down at her.

"And what can I do for you, young lady?" he said, his voice a pleasing, humoured growl.

"May I entreat you to make one more run tonight, sir?" she said, keeping her voice high and sweet.

Hudson narrowed his eyes and pushed back his woollen cap to scratch at his balding pate. "What would a little slip of a thing like you need that for?"

If she had been physically able to cry, she would have summoned the tears. She couldn't, though, so she settled for a slight quivering of both lip and tone as she said "my papa," inwardly pleased at the distress she had been able to bring to those two words. "He was working out in Saskatchewan, sir. He suffered an accidental gunshot wound and he…" She paused, sucked in an unnecessary breath, added a quaver to her voice to make it sound as though it was a struggle to get the next words out. "…And he…uh…he died, sir."

Hudson dropped to his haunches, his face softening, the pipe removed. He put a hand on her shoulder. Chloe did not like to be touched, but she suffered through it to continue the façade. "Ah, poor, sweet kid. I'm so sorry for your loss. May god rest his soul."

Oh how those last five sounds grated on her. Still, she held her reaction back, allowing only the ones this captain would expect. She dropped her gaze to the deck, checking for his shadow. "Thank you," she said, her voice barely above a whisper.

She noticed the slight pooling of darkness at his feet. He had a shadow. Faint, but there.

Yes, it is definitely just me, she thought. *Probably not enough to worry about, but I should remain cautious.*

Hudson's voice interrupted her thoughts. "So, what do you need my boat for?"

"His casket…my papa's just come in on the Grand Trunk Railway. Mama's busy with the young'uns back home, and sent me to see to it he got home." She raised her face up to meet his gaze. He smelled of wet wool, sweat, and pipe tobacco. "Mama wants to lay him to rest before the snow flies, sir."

She'd said her piece. Now it was up to him.

"My boat's supposed to go in dry dock in the mornin'," he said. "My crew's lookin' forward to a hot meal and their beds."

Probably looking forward to sharing that bed with a woman willing to rent herself out for a couple of hours, too, Chloe thought, but did not say.

She waited.

Hudson rolled it over in his mind.

She watched him carefully. She'd rather not have to use her Voice to coerce him.

She watched him glance at the sky, thick with grey clouds. He scratched at his thick beard, muttered, "prob'ly gonna snow," and shook his head slightly.

He slipped his hand from her shoulder and she knew he'd made his decision, and it wasn't in her favour.

"I can pay," she said. She dipped a hand into her pocket and pulled out some money. "I've got fifteen dollars." Saying it like she didn't know it was far too much for a single trip the length of the lake. Saying it like it wasn't more than Hudson's crew would make in a week.

Captain Hudson's eyes widened, then narrowed back down.

"It's five o'clock now," he said, more to himself than her. "We could prob'ly be back by no later than two, countin' for off-loading."

Chloe kept her mouth shut.

"Boat could use some repairs…" He didn't say they'd be costly, but they would.

He placed his hand on her shoulder again.

"Prob'ly don't need the full crew…" he said.

She let the decision come to him.

"And if I put the word out, might even get a few more travellers."

He gave her shoulder another, hopefully final, squeeze, and released his hand.

"All right, honey," he said. "I'll round up a couple of my guys and get the word out. You can get your papa down to the *Mayflower* in the next hour or so?"

"Yes, sir," she said.

"You're a resourceful little thing, ain't ya?" he said. "All well and fine then. We'll catch a quick bite and, in two hours, we'll be on our way." He stood, his knees cracking with the effort.

"Thank you ever so much, Captain Hudson." She handed over the money.

"More than welcome, honey," he said. "You got someone travellin' with you tonight? Aside from your papa, I mean?"

"No, sir," Chloe said. "It will just be me heading home with my papa." *Don't ask who 'my papa' is, Hudson. Don't ask where we live. Don't you dare.*

Hudson only looked down at the money in his hands, nodded, said, "sorry for your loss, honey," and turned away.

You're far more concerned with your unexpected gain than any loss I may be suffering, Captain Hudson. Still, you're doing what I need you to do, so we both gain from this, don't we?

As she watched him climb the hill to the diner, she kept her smile to herself. There were other boats that made the same journey, but none travelling with the same regularity. This had been one of the key factors to this plan, and it was going to work.

She'd get there. Her and her First.

Now, the First only had to do her part once they got there.

CHAPTER THREE

C HLOE MADE HER way through the grey afternoon to the barn where the First and the casket were waiting. She checked carefully before she moved off the road, to ensure no one was watching. Personally, she didn't think a young girl would be questioned for walking toward a barn on a cold November afternoon, but the First had insisted on diligence, so she did her best to comply.

The First.

Chloe did not like the leader of their Clutch, which caused some friction. *If I'm honest,* she thought, *if someone held a stake to my heart, I'd have to admit I likely prefer the company of shifters to her presence.* Not that she'd actually met any shifters. But she'd heard some stories.

Every member of the Clutch knew the true name of every other Clutch member, making secrets impossible. So, it was also no secret that the First held nothing but contempt for Chloe as well.

Still, in their short history of nine decades or so—well before that upstart from the Carpathian Mountains showed up—Chloe had been able to distinguish herself enough to rise to the level of Second in the Clutch.

That threatened the First. And because there were no secrets in the Clutch, they all knew it. It seemed strange to be told she was the "up and coming" leader after almost a century of Clutch membership, but there it was.

She pulled on the door of the barn, opening it only enough to slip through, the weathered wood rough but pleasant under her hands as she pulled it closed again. The pleasant feeling faded as she turned to face the First of the Clutch.

"Well, Glory? What have you accomplished?" The First addressed her by the etymological meaning of her name. Chloe meant Verdant Glory. Names held power. Using the original name meaning was equivalent to the human handshake: it meant there was no threat here, no ulterior motive.

Chloe took a knee and held her head back and off to one side, offering her throat. "First," she said.

The First made the appropriate gesture, and Chloe stood. She took a hard look at the woman who led their Clutch. Standing at full height, and still at the size and shape of a human girl of nine or ten, Chloe was only a shade below the First's eye level. Ileen—whose name meant "Light," and only that was used in place of her honorific, never her real name—was several centuries older than Chloe, and looked like she was in her late twenties—ancient for their race. There were the beginnings of lines around her eyes, at the corners of her mouth. Her breasts had started their inevitable sag. But for all of that, her only concession to advancing age was a bloom of grey dusting the curls that framed her forehead, a small bit of frost in the mahogany of her hair.

"I have secured transport on the *Mayflower* for myself and the casket." She nodded to where an unadorned pine box lay in a bed of hay. "As agreed, they believe the casket carries my father."

"Was coercion required?" The First's tone told her she knew the answer.

"No," Chloe said. "The payment was adequate." She knew her First had expected her to fail at navigating the vagaries of human communication. Had that occurred, Chloe would have used her ability to push compliance on the captain. Chloe knew this was not the answer she'd anticipated, and that it would irk her.

The First's eyes flared briefly, but her face remained stonily impassive. "Very well," the First said.

High praise. Chloe kept the smirk from angling her lips. She pulled a pocket watch from a pocket. "The boat leaves in just over an hour. We should get you inside and get the casket to the *Mayflower.*"

Two other Clutch members lifted the lid of the casket away. Inside, there was a thick layer of soil from the town of Vilni, enough that the First should experience only minor discomfort on the journey.

Of course, she lies prone and comfortable, while I face the rigours of the water crossing.

The First stepped into the casket, gripped the rough edges of the box, and settled herself down. She gave the two others a small nod and they replaced the lid and nailed it down, the sounds of hammers on wood and iron harsh in the quiet of the evening.

When they completed the task, the two lifted the casket and placed it gently on the bed of the horse-driven carriage. They both dropped to a knee and bared their throats — *a rather stupid, futile gesture, considering she is sealed inside the casket,* Chloe thought — then one disappeared out the back of the barn, and the other beckoned for Chloe as he climbed to the front of the carriage and took the reins.

They could have used a truck — they had the means — but the First did not want to draw undue attention through any show of wealth, imagined or real. The fifteen dollars had been more than enough.

The driver snapped the reins, making a clicking noise and, squinting under the blinding sheen of the cloud-covered sky, they headed to the dock.

Chapter Four

THE CASKET WAS settled into a corner of the box-like boat's storage area, and Chloe sat in the passenger area on a hard bench, waiting on other passengers and the inevitable start to the journey in—she checked her pocket watch again—roughly twenty minutes.

The boat wasn't even moving as yet, but Chloe felt the disorientation and a strange flexing of her guts at just being on the water. It was unpleasant for a being that truly felt no discomfort aside from hunger. It was going to be a long, unpleasant wait, followed by a longer, more unpleasant journey.

And Chloe was going to have a lot of time to think about it.

The passenger area was quiet until about ten minutes before departure. That's when three more sets of passengers came on.

The first was an older couple, sweetly holding hands. They moved to a bench directly across from Chloe, and the gentleman tipped his hat to her before pulling it off and dusting the bench before his wife sat down. She gave him an appreciative smile and he sat close beside her. When they'd made themselves comfortable, he took her hand once again in his, patting it gently with the other.

The second were two younger men in worn and oft-repaired clothes, bearded and calloused. They took a bench to the same side as the elderly couple, but off to one end, lighting up hand-rolled cigarettes once they were settled.

The last was a father with a son of about ten. The father sat at the opposite end from the smoking men, the old couple between the two. The son dutifully sat beside him, then almost immediately stood again to wander the area and look out the windows. The father looked as though ready to rebuke the child, but then closed his mouth, pulled a pipe and a tobacco pouch from a pocket, and proceeded to fill the pipe's bowl.

Interesting that all six of them unconsciously took seats away from me. I wonder if they're even aware of that?

Chloe spared each of them surreptitious glances when she could. She did this unhurriedly, not making it obvious. The older couple was harmless, interested only in their devotion to each other. She caught their eyes in a more open glance and got smiles from both and gave one in return. They would pose no problems.

The younger pair of men, while rough of clothing, language, and demeanour, also appeared only interested in getting to their destination. They were quiet in their conversation, and—from listening in—they were only looking for enough work to get some meals in their bellies and more tobacco, then it would be off to the next opportunity. Given the right circumstances, they could be trouble, but it wouldn't be here.

The father and child, however, she couldn't get a read on. The father paid little attention to the boy, and the boy never really checked in with the father as a normal child would in an unfamiliar situation.

Then again, Chloe could hardly be considered an expert in human behaviour. Maybe this was a familiar situation. Maybe they made this trip often. She resolved to keep an eye on the father. Obviously the boy would not be an issue.

She tried to relax as the boat's paddle wheels started to dig against the water, attempting to make herself more comfortable and, failing, let her head rest against the wall, and closed her eyes. Her stomach roiled and bucked now that they were in motion. Her eyes didn't seem to track well. Her mind spun with an unfocused panic, the thought of nothing but water underneath her, unsolid, untrustworthy, more than willing to swallow her, yet not kill her.

She resigned herself to getting through the next boring, uncomfortable three hours of this trip.

Chapter Five

CHLOE WOKE FIRST to sensation, then to words spat harshly, landing like hail.

She opened her eyes and initially felt more than saw the boy sitting beside her. Close beside her. Her sight still rolled slightly, her eyes not able to track properly with the movement over water. But yes, the child sat beside her.

Then, from the seats across from her, she heard the boy's father growl, "Get back over here, you little shit." The public vulgarity — despite the rough-and-tumble town they'd begun their passage from — was shocking in its casual bluntness.

The older woman pursed her lips, and her husband turned to the father, his mouth opening to say something, likely to berate him, but closed again. Chloe shot a quick glance at the father and saw why. He was leaning forward, elbows on knees, hands clenched tightly into fists. He looked like a stick of dynamite, ready to explode.

Turning to the boy, she locked eyes. The child was terrified, that much was obvious, and the expression on his face told her he was looking, if not for salvation, at least for protection.

"Don't you look at her, Roderick, she ain't gonna save you," the father said. "You mind your father and get over here. *Now.*"

Trying to defuse the situation, Chloe said, "It's okay, I don't mind if he—"

A single finger on the father's right fist popped out, pointed to the floor in front of him. "Right. Now."

Without taking her eyes off the man, she set a comforting hand on the boy's shoulder, gently pushing him. In a low voice, she said, "You better listen to your father, Roderick." She didn't try and coerce him, but if he didn't move, she would, if only to spare him a beating.

The boy sighed softly, stood, and trod slowly toward his father, the man's finger still indicating the patch of floor in front of him. When he got within reach, his father shot an arm out, caught the boy in a violent grip, and wrenched him over and down to the bench beside him. Roderick's too-long hair flopped over his face as he sat quietly, resignedly, staring at the floor.

One of the smoking men pulled his cigarette from his lips and stood.

"What?" the father said, also standing. "What are you going to do?" He stabbed a finger toward his son, who flinched. "He's my son. *My* son. *My* property to do with as I please. What are you going to do?"

The other smoker tugged on the standing man's sleeve. "Sit down, Kent," he said. "It ain't none of our concern."

When Chloe flicked her gaze to the elderly couple, the man seemed to mirror Roderick, simply staring wide-eyed at the floor, his hands clasping and unclasping each other. His wife stared out at nothing, tears sliding down her cheeks.

Kent yanked his arm away from his tugging friend and reluctantly sat down. The cigarette trailed smoke from between his fingers, forgotten.

It grew quiet on the boat then, with only the wind and the water and the chugging engines and the rhythmic sounds of the paddle wheel to fill the uncomfortable void. The younger men smoked in silence, the older couple kept a frustrated silence, the father stared furiously out the windows, Roderick kneaded his woollen mittens as he flicked quick glances at his father.

At any other time, despite having no love for these people or their filthy offspring, she would have been happy to teach this foul-mouthed beast a lesson about property and respect. Then she would have torn his throat out and consumed his blood while he died a permanent death.

But this was not that time.

Chloe closed her eyes once again and tried to tell herself it was none of her concern.

Chapter Six

THE FIRST SNOW began to fall just as the sun dipped below the horizon. Chloe was happy the sun was finally setting for, despite the blanket of thick clouds, she still felt its presence, a constant, unwelcome adversary through the first part of the voyage. It had not helped her misery.

However, as the darkness set in, and the lights on the boat were turned up, Chloe was dismayed by the lack of stars. She enjoyed the night, but it was always the stars that entranced her. Distant suns, or so she had read, but distant enough to have only the effect of curiosity on her, no discomfort. It was the lack of stars this evening that caused the discomfort.

Still, the night was her time. Despite the dearth of stars, there was the mitigating effect, an easing, however slight, of her misery. She could hold her gaze somewhat. She could push through the fog of her mind. She could ignore the tempest in her belly.

She could do this.

As the snow became more insistent, it was blown hard into the boat by increasingly buffeting winds. She stood — quickly checking on Roderick, who appeared to have fallen asleep on the bench beside his father — and moved to the door leading to the small walkway on the boat deck. She pushed on the door. The wind pushed back. She applied more force and opened the door to a fury of wind and snow and noise. She barely heard the older woman telling her to take care as she stepped to the railing.

Despite the light leaking from the windows down the length of the boat, she could see nothing of the shore. There were points between the two wider bowls where the Kwanashishing narrowed to a couple of dozen yards in width, more a river than a lake, and points where it widened to just over a mile across. She guessed they were in the narrows, but she couldn't tell. All was black, broken only by falling snow.

As though the *Mayflower* was sailing through the night sky, the snowflakes like stars whirling around them.

The temperature had also dropped noticeably. It didn't cause Chloe any discomfort whatsoever, but she'd learned over the decades that others expected it to, so she had to act like it did.

She pulled open the door again, and stepped back into the room with a swirl of snow.

"Shut the damn door," the father said, making Roderick flinch out of his slumber. "This ain't a damn barn, girlie."

She ignored the man, pushed the door shut, faked a shiver more to get the dusting of snow off her than anything, and took up her place on the bench again.

As she brushed the last of the snow off her forearms and shoulders, she heard the soft, pleasant voice of the old woman who sat across from her. "Looks to be getting a mite blustery out there," she said. She gave Chloe a warm smile. Chloe knew the woman was just trying to show some kindness to the young girl travelling on her own, after the tongue lashing from Roderick's father.

"It is," she said, remembering to keep her voice soft and high. Ileen would not be pleased if she found out Chloe had used the Voice. Transitioning between the Voice and a normal, human voice was still not automatic for her. It would likely be a few more decades before she wrestled it under control.

"I hope we'll be okay," the old woman said. "We still have a couple of hours to go, don't we?" She gave her husband a hopeful look.

"Don't you fuss," he said, patting her hand. "This old tub's been plying these waters many a year, and nothing's gone wrong yet, has it?"

"It got stove in a few years back when it hit a log or somethin'," one of the younger men said. Kent. His name meant *just* or *righteous*. "Boat started sinkin', but they saved it. Don't think it's passed for safety since, though."

"Oh dear," the old woman said.

"We'll be fine," her husband said, shooting the younger man a warning look. "Don't you fret."

"You don't have to sit all the way over there all by your lonesome," the old woman said. Chloe figured she was looking for someone to comfort to take her mind off the weather, but Chloe was reluctant to sit anywhere she couldn't keep an eye on Roderick's father.

"Thank you," she said, then let a hint of Voice creep into her tone. "But I'm fine here. We'll all be fine."

Kent looked like he was going to say something else, and she didn't trust it to be mind-easing, so she gave him a look and the smallest shake of her head. He closed his mouth, and angled his head to look out the window.

The old woman sat back, some of the lines of worry smoothing away from her face and, because she seemed a bit more calm, her husband echoed her, sitting back, his expression relaxing, but not his grip on his wife's hand.

CHAPTER SEVEN

IT MUST HAVE been the increasing fury of the storm, but Roderick woke silently, eyeing his father who had fallen asleep sometime in the past hour. Chloe eyed the man as well. He slept on, completely oblivious to the turmoil just beyond the walls of the boat.

Chloe watched the boy's movements. She could read a lot into them.

He lifted his legs up, then swung them out and down to the floor, his feet silently greeting the surface. He did this instead of simply sliding his legs over the bench and down.

He eased himself up to a sitting position slowly, taking his time, making no noise above a soft rustle of cloth as he moved.

And through it all, his eyes remained locked on his father's face. His eyes, rolling under his eyelids. His slack-jawed mouth, huffing out deep breaths.

This is how he always wakes, she knew. *Instantly alert to where his father is, and the state he's in. It's a survival tactic.*

The boy stood with a minimum of movement, graceful as a dancer, and placed his steps carefully and deliberately as he increased the distance between himself and the sleeping dragon that was his father.

He came toward Chloe, a worried expression on his face.

Probably a little bit due to the storm, and a whole lot to do with daddy. She patted the bench next to her.

He doesn't get to play with other kids, she thought. *So the fact that he's in a room with someone he thinks is his age is enough of a temptation to risk his father's rage.*

He sat with the same care as he had displayed when he left the bench beside his father. When he was settled, he simply sat, looking at her. She realized that, while he wanted her company, he didn't really know what to do now that he had it.

And that made her wonder. *How starved for companionship does someone have to be to risk being beaten just so they can experience it for a bit?*

She looked at Roderick with different eyes then.

You're the bravest person I know, she realized.

I can't do anything about the storm, or his father, but I can try and take his mind off both. She pitched her voice just above a whisper. "Your name's Roderick?"

He nodded, but then made a face.

"You don't like your name?"

He shook his head.

"Well, I think it's a fine name," she said. "I guess I'm not crazy about my name either," she said.

He cocked his head to the side.

"It's Chloe," she said, then felt an immediate flutter in her chest. She hadn't spoken her name aloud for almost eighty years, and she damned well hadn't offered it up willingly to anyone but the First, ever.

Names were powerful. Knowing someone's name—especially their full name—bound them to you.

The First of the Clutch had that right. But no one else. It was the first lesson taught upon admittance to the Clutch.

And yet, here I am, casually tossing it out to a child.

At the sound of her name, he smiled. "Ah, you like my name?"

He nodded. Emphatically. He smiled broadly, and it transformed him.

"You don't speak much, do you?"

He shook his head no.

"Do you speak at all?"

Another no.

"Well then," she said, slathering a layer of teasing over her tone, "however will I know what you like to be called?"

He held his hand out, giving her a look.

She held her own out, mimicking him, eyebrows raised in question.

He traced a letter on her palm. It tickled somewhat, and she laughed as her fingers curled involuntarily.

"R," she said.

He nodded and traced a circle.

"O."

A nod. Another letter.

"R," she said. "Again."

A nod. A last letter.

"Y," she said. "Rory?"

He nodded.

"Rory," she said, trying it out, rolling it on her tongue. "I like it," she proclaimed.

She took his hand with her outstretched one. "Do you know what Rory means?"

No.

She released his hand, and ruffled his red thatch of hair. "It means 'Red King,'" she said. He raised his eyebrows.

"Yes, really. Red King." Then she laughed at the delighted expression on his face. "It suits you, doesn't it?"

He nodded.

Then she watched his eyes flick to her right, and the delight fall from his face.

"What the hell kind of shite are you filling the boy's head with?"

Rory's father lifted each of them off the bench, a calloused hand around each of their forearms.

But he stumbled a bit then, as the beleaguered boat started to list.

PART TWO
STORM

"I am all in a sea of wonders. I doubt, I fear, I think strange things, which I dare not confess to my own soul."

DRACULA
BRAM STOKER

CHAPTER EIGHT

"WHAT THE HELL?" the father said.

He released both Chloe and Rory to throw both hands out at the wall and spread his legs, just to maintain his balance.

Chloe fell back to the bench, flinging a hand out to steady Rory.

And through it all, the angle of the listing boat just kept increasing, as though a massive hand had caught it and was tugging it down.

Kent, his smoking partner, and the old couple were making the usual inarticulate sounds of panic just as one of the boat's crew came in with three life preservers. He threw them to the older couple, and one to Kent. In his own panic, they were likely the first three passengers he'd even noticed.

The older man said "there's more of these coming?" as he held up the preserver.

"No, sir, that's all we've got, and we left the lifeboat back in New Hope." Then he ran back out to the deck.

The man gave his wife a quick look and she nodded. Then he released his grip on their bench and awkwardly slid downslope toward Chloe and Rory. "You take them," he said. "We've lived a good long time. You deserve the same chance."

Rory's father had slid away from them, too busy looking out the windows to notice what had happened. Chloe quickly fastened the life preserver to Rory's trembling body, the fabric and cork stiff and difficult, the straps awkward. The old man assisted her where he could.

Chloe grabbed Rory by both shoulders. "Hang on to the bench. I'll be right back."

She caught the old man's forearm and climbed the canted floor with him, delivering him back to his wife, furiously clutching at her own bench. "Thank you, young lady," he said.

"Thank *you*," she said, meaning it.

Then she stumbled over to Kent, and—not pausing to contemplate what watery hell she was actually consigning herself to—held out the other life jacket. "Give this to your buddy," she said. "I can swim."

She couldn't. Moving water was the enemy, but she too had lived a good long time.

Chloe refused to question where this sudden and disgusting weakness, this surprising altruism toward the humans, came from. Knowing full well that it was Rory.

Kent looked like he was hesitating, so she shoved it into his chest and then scrambled and slid back across the room to Rory.

All was confusion. Rory's father was yelling. Kent and his friend were yelling. From behind her, she heard the captain yelling to dump the casket in the water, and her first thought was, *No!*

But when she turned back to Rory, his father had made it back to him and was desperately tearing at the jacket, trying to pull it from the boy.

She brought every ounce of Voice to bear as she commanded, **"No."**

He looked confused, and his fingers still scrabbled at the straps ineffectually, but he'd stopped all violent motion.

And then she had an idea. Maybe spin this altruism to her benefit.

Lifting her voice above the din, commanding them all, she said, "**Come with me.**"

They followed.

She gave them no choice.

CHAPTER NINE

B Y THE TIME the seven of them were out on the ice and snow-slicked deck, a third of the boat was under the madly heaving surface of Lake Kwanashishing. The massive waves weren't sinking the boat, they were devouring it.

Three of the deckhands had muscled the casket to the edge of the portside deck, but the wind, the snow, the ice, the waves, the angle of the boat, and the tossing about made it virtually impossible for them to cast it off the side.

Chloe was also feeling the effects of the violent water. She hadn't thrown up in over eighty years, but she felt like she might now.

She swallowed back the taste of blood and bile, strode forward, one hand on the guardrail, one on the banister fixed to the outer wall. When she got close, and not trusting her throat enough to not vomit as she attempted to use the Voice, she simply grabbed the deckhand by the back of his slicker and wrenched him away from the casket. Then she braced herself as best she could, caught both hands under the rough wood, and heaved the damnable thing over the side.

The waves did the rest of the work, pushing it back toward her six travelling companions.

"Jump in. Grab the casket."

They all did, with no hesitation at the thought of the near-freezing water temperature. Chloe, on the other hand, had to fight against the rejection of her own body's reflexes. Everything in her was telling her it's *running water you can't cross running water you can't you can't you can't.*

Spitting bile, she jumped.

And caught the casket.

CHAPTER TEN

EXTREME COLD DID not affect a vampire. Nor did extreme heat. Snow, rain, and wind could similarly be ignored. Chloe had felt no true physical discomfort in her entire life.

She thought she had, two hours ago, back at the start of this damnable voyage. But now she knew the truth. All that had come before was mere unpleasantry compared to this. Previous to here and now, she had suffered nothing.

Until this moment.

Submerged in the black water of Lake Kwanashishing, arms lashed to the casket of her First, head barely above the waves, the lake needled into her, the cold pushing out everything but pain. The cold surrounded her, bit at her, burrowed into her, tightened and froze her muscles, made her bones grind against each other. Her eyes burned, her ears roared, her jaws clamped in the futile attempt to shut out the water invading her mouth. She couldn't feel her fingers, her hands, her feet.

If she could die, this is what it would feel like. She couldn't even shiver, as her body had long ago lost that most basic of human instincts.

Damnable running water.

She forced herself to focus outward, not inward. Through the swirl of the snow, and the heaving waters, Rory clung to the other side, directly facing her, eyes wide with terror, his red hair frozen into white spikes of ice. His father had also made it, holding on only a foot to her left. Two forms bobbed up near the head of the casket. Kent and his friend. Had to be.

The old man and woman were nowhere to be seen.

Kent must have seen her scanning around for them. He yelled, "They didn't make it."

She barely heard him and could only nod in response, hoping he saw.

Though none of them were doing well, the storm tossing them about like ants on a cork, it was Rory's father who looked to be in danger of slipping away. Aside from Chloe, he was the only one without a life jacket.

They were both in the most danger right now. But she thought she might have a short-term solution that could help them both.

Chloe carefully removed, then replaced, the position of each numb hand to pull herself closer to the father. For his part, he didn't seem to notice. He was looking at something behind her.

His teeth were chattering with the cold, but she still made out his, "Jesus, Mary, and Joseph."

She shot a glance at Kent and his friend, and she knew that the *Mayflower* had just slipped beneath the surface. It was gone.

This was her chance. And in her current state, she couldn't even trust her Voice.

She lunged, wrapping her hands around the father's neck, both to hold on to him and to try and disguise what she was about to do.

Not that anyone would be able to make it out in the darkness, lightened only by falling snow, like dying stars.

Chapter Eleven

H E WAS TOO cold and too surprised to react, and her numb fingers were able to thrust his head skyward, baring his unshaven neck.

Chloe hated it when they didn't shave.

Still, she didn't hesitate, only drove her mouth forward, tearing at the soft flesh of his neck. The Eternal Hunger, normally banked warm coals inside her, now roared to full blaze, demanding sustenance.

Gaining access to someone's blood was never a neat affair. It was harsh, shocking, violent, and messy. Chloe's teeth sunk through his skin, into the muscle. She felt the lump of his Adam's apple working up and down under her nose as she finally opened that vital artery, thick with warm, rich, oxygenated blood. She swallowed bits of skin and lumps of muscle and slushy lake water along with the jetting blood, and immediately felt her body warm only a bit at first, then quickening as she fed, the numbness retreating from her hands, her feet, her sickness abating and the warmth of her sex responding.

As much as she wanted to drain this bastard, the Eternal Hunger howling in her breast for more, she needed him.

So, she took what she required.

Then she took just a little more.

She felt him letting go, and she couldn't let that happen just yet. **"Hold on,"** she commanded and, though he was weak, though he was dying, he obeyed, and his fingers crabbed with feeble strength at the slick, rough boards of the casket. She eyed the two men at the head of the casket, but they were still preoccupied with the loss of the boat, and with just hanging on.

Chloe lifted her arm to her face, grabbed at her coat sleeve with her fangs and tore it open, baring her forearm. She opened herself up, laying the network of veins and arteries open. It would take a bit longer in her weakened state to heal back up, but necessary to do what she needed.

She pushed her gored arm into the father's mouth—his name was Bertram, but she didn't believe him to be the bright raven his name suggested—but he didn't drink.

Damn it, Chloe. She'd done too much damage to his throat.

She pulled her arm from his slack mouth and pressed directly against the open hole in his neck. While his heart still beat, it would seep into his bloodstream and leak down his broken esophagus to his stomach.

The casket continued to bob and bounce, and the thickening snow hissed as it hit the water. While she waited for her blood to work its magic on Bertram, she yelled to the others.

"We've got to push for shore."

"What?"

"**SHORE**," she bellowed, feeling the wood vibrate with the bass tone of the command. **"Push the casket to shore."**

The three men—Bertram surprisingly among them—and the boy began kicking their feet in unison for the unseen shore.

She took a moment to examine Bertram. It was hard to tell in these conditions, but the wound at his neck appeared smaller, and he held the casket with a bit more strength.

It would have to do.

She pulled her bloodied arm away, and only then did she look over to Rory.

Who, while still kicking, was staring back at her.

He'd seen it all.

Chapter Twelve

"Rory," she barked, more from surprise than anything. *He'd seen.*

"We need to get you out of the water."

He continued to silently stare at her. Only involuntary shivers made him blink.

He'd seen.

Still, he was small, and the water would leech the heat right out of his bones faster than the adults'.

"Come on," she said, throwing an arm across the casket. "Grab my hand."

Rory just clung to the wood.

"Damn it," she said, but only to herself. She really didn't want to coerce him. Not him. Not Rory.

Still, she didn't have much choice. **"Grab my hand."** He immediately reached out, even as his eyes widened ever further. She pulled, and he got one leg up on the top of the box. Kent reached out and hefted him further to the middle of the surface.

"Now, hold on." Rory hooked his feet around the edges and clenched his small fists around the wooden corners.

Chloe allowed herself to relax then, if only for a moment. She let her legs go loose and flow with the opposing currents of icy water, letting the three men do the work. She would help, but she also needed to save her strength.

Because the first of two thoughts struck her, hitting her like a bolt of lightning.

The first was that this storm had come up too quickly and too violently to have been natural. She had seen storms, and she had seen *storms*, but this one didn't feel right. She was coming around to the idea that it had been manipulated. It had been pushed to greater calamity. And there were only two things she knew of that could possibly make that happen.

Both of them held by the audience they were travelling to meet.

The wolves.

Then, with the thought of the meeting, the second lightning bolt of realization crackled through her frenzied mind. Her First was still in this damned box they were pushing to shore.

She was very likely awake. Chloe couldn't think of a reason why she wouldn't be.

But with the running water, and her tossing about in the casket, she was also very likely not strong enough to save herself.

The thoughts swirled around her mind as the snow and wind-whipped water swirled around her head. Then something else happened that pushed all the thoughts aside.

It started with a needling sensation in her scalp, that Chloe put down to the cold. But it crept along her head, then down her neck, to her shoulders, arms, lower…

She got a sense of impending danger. Her muscles stiffened. Her jaw clenched. She couldn't even open her eyes. She was barely able to reach a shaking hand out to Rory's and clutch at it, just to feel contact with something living.

She couldn't think. Her body was tightened and twisted almost into a fetal position. She could only push out a moan that rang too low for anyone to hear. She wanted to die. Something wanted to consume her, to pull her apart and scatter her.

It went on and on, digging deep into her muscles, her bones, her brain. It pushed into her, pushing out all coherent thought, leaving only pain behind.

She trembled and shook and focused on the singular sensation of Rory's cold hand in hers.

It went on and on, never stopping, never abating.

On and on.

On and on.

And then, as a breath snuffed a candle's flame, it stopped, leaving only whisps of ache in muscle and mind.

It took many minutes more for Chloe to painstakingly unclench every muscle in her body, to unbend her fingers from Rory's hand, to allow the trembling to subside, to let the overwhelming thoughts of danger and doom slide to the side and allow more rational thought to return.

It took longer still for Chloe to understand what had happened.

They'd done it.

They'd passed under the boundary, slipping under the small anomaly out here in the water.

If we'd been in the boat, we wouldn't have made it, she realized. *We had to be well submerged in the running water.*

They'd made it through.

Then came the echoing thunder of the final realization…

Now that they'd survived the boundary crossing, it was up to Chloe to save both herself and her First.

CHAPTER THIRTEEN

ERTRAM WAS COMPLETELY under her thrall since she'd fed him with her blood. He was kicking as steadily as could be hoped for under the current conditions. He had another layer of snow and ice coating his head and arms. Chloe was about to remind him yet again to break it clear, but she noticed that it was melting and sliding off.

Damnation, she thought. *He's sweating. That means the change is coming soon.*

That meant he was going to die first. Then he would come back.

She wasn't that worried about him. He'd continue until he couldn't anymore, like a clock's mainspring winding down. With what she'd pulled from his mind when she pulled his blood from his body, she didn't care when he stopped. He had to die to change.

She'd deal with him then, and leave him for the lake to claim.

But Kent and his travelling partner, though desperate to reach shore, were flagging. She did her best to not use her Voice on them because she saw the two of them were keeping each other going, each pushing the other to go a little further, kick a few more times.

She sure as hell she didn't want to feed from them or turn them, despite the gut-clenching hunger roiling inside her. Unlike Bertram, they seemed like decent folk.

Decent folk? Chloe, what's the matter with you? She shook her head clear of the errant thought.

Chloe reached up and put a hand on Rory. He was shivering. His lips were darkening. Under the frail light of snow-blown darkness, she saw well enough to know his lips were turning blue.

Not good. We've got to get out of this lake.

She raised her voice—maybe a little bit of Voice thrown in just to get it to carry, but not enough to coerce—and yelled, "What's your name?" to Kent's partner.

"Zeke," he yelled back.

Zeke. Ezekiel.

"Zeke," she said. "I'm Glory."

"Pleased to meet ya," he said, and even managed a grin. "Even if it ain't under the best of conditions."

"Your name," she said. "Did you know it means—"

"God's strength," he said. "Yeah."

"Then I am to be saved by both a righteous man," she said, pointing to Kent, "and a strong man," she said, pointing to Zeke.

"We're gonna do our best," Kent said.

It was enough to spur them on a little longer.

Names, she thought. *They truly do have power.*

Chapter Fourteen

A HALF HOUR later, Bertram let out a sound. Not quite a moan, not quite a whine, and not quite a sigh, but somehow all three. Chloe watched his body lose all tension, and his hands slipped from the wood's surface.

Bertram was dead. He just didn't quite realize it yet.

Kent and Zeke were locked into a mindless rhythm of kicking. They weren't talking, they might not even be completely conscious anymore, but they were still pushing the casket implacably toward shore.

Rory had slipped into semi-consciousness as well, barely holding on.

So Chloe had been the only one to see Bertram release his hold and slip deeper into the heaving water.

She had to work quickly.

Ensuring she had a good grip, she twisted her body and caught Bertram between her scissoring legs. Then she slowly, painfully, worked her way around the corner of the casket, away from Kent and Zeke.

Vampires didn't do well with running bodies of water. But Chloe had no clue whether Bertram might resurrect and, in a day, or in a decade, somehow find his way out of this hellish liquid prison.

She had to ensure that would not occur. Not tomorrow, not ten years from now, not ever.

Maintaining a tenuous hold on the casket with one hand,

she used the other to haul upward on the waterlogged body of Rory's father. When she had him roughly face-to-face with her, she pushed his head back and once again brought her teeth to bear on his neck.

This time, however, the intent was not to feed, but to separate head from neck.

She bit, pulled, and spat the dead flesh into the uncaring water. Then, with the casket heaving in the waves, and the snow covering everything, she did it again.

Then, again.

Then, again.

Finally, there was little left but some tough sinew and the spine. She grasped the spine and tore it back, bending it in half, then attacked it with her teeth again, the cartilage slick and unyielding under her fangs.

With her one hand twisting the head this way and that, and her mouth knifing through every obstacle, suddenly her mouth flooded with the salty, metallic taste of spinal fluid, and she bit down hard, crunching through the last of the bone and cartilage, and the head came off and she lost it to the waves.

No great loss.

She spit Bertram's spinal fluid out of her mouth, dipped her mouth in the water, and spit again to clear the fragments of bone and gristle.

She kept his body pinched between her thighs. She would give the head time to travel its final path before she'd release the body as far away from it as she could manage.

Glancing around, she squinted her eyes against the snow and spray. *Is that…?*

She crab-walked her way back around the casket, yelling for Kent and Zeke.

"Oh, thank the Lord," Zeke said. "I thought we'd lost you."

"No," she yelled. "We did lose Rory's father." She didn't mention that she still held most of him tight between her thighs. "I went round the side to see if I could catch sight of shore."

"I can't see a blamed thing," Kent said.

"It's there," she said, pointing over Rory's prone, shivering body. "Straight ahead. No more than a couple of hundred feet."

Kent, with more vigour than he'd shown in the previous two hours, shot a look around his side of the casket. She saw him squint, then bring a shielding hand up to his brow as though to block the light of the sun. But it was the snow he was blocking.

He lowered his hand. "I think she might be right. Can't rightly see nothing in this storm, but if it is, the rest is duck soup."

Not another word was said. The two men leaned into their task with renewed energy.

Chloe gave it another ten minutes, then let the rest of Bertram loose and kicked at the water herself.

Along the way, she closed out all outside distractions and focused on linking her mind with her First in the casket.

Chapter Fifteen

ILEEN WAS FURIOUS.

She'd been trapped in this godsdamned casket for the past three hours and, while the darkness and the Vilni soil she lay in was a comfort, she knew the second she was moved from dry land and set on the boat. Her stomach had lurched, and her head began to pulse with a hammering rhythm. Initially, it was almost a novelty, having not had a headache—having not experienced *any* aches or pains—for so long she'd forgotten what they felt like.

She soon remembered, however, and the novelty wore off quickly. The pain, though, only worsened from a minor squall to a raging storm.

Much like, she gathered from the ever-increasing howl of wind and the tossing of the boat, the weather outside continued to worsen.

Why? she wondered. *Why did it have to happen this way?* Crossing the godsdamned lake of running water—anathema to most supernatural beings, hell to a vampire—just to meet with fucking *dogs*.

If it wasn't for the damned curse…

And the luck of the mongrels, finding both the infernal Book and the Staff of Solomon, old when the universe was young, thought long-lost. Finding both as though by some divine or dreadful intervention.

Somehow, both fell into their unworthy paws, and left the

proud, far superior race coming to grovel to them.

Oh, how it boiled her blood.

And now, it came down to Ileen, stuck in this claustrophobic casket, blind and helpless to her fate.

Still, she kept her anxiety at bay until she felt the box she was trapped in slide first one way, then another, slamming into unseen obstacles and throwing her around like dice in the hand of a desperate gambler.

She tried reaching out to Chloe, who was supposed to be watching out for her First's safety and failing miserably. But with the violence of the movement, the arcing shots of pain running from her temples to her neck, and the fact that she didn't exactly know where the whelp was situated, she found it impossible to locate her charge. Failing just as miserably as Chloe.

When she heard the command to dump the casket overboard, just as she felt the boat severely listing to one side, she skipped directly past anxiety and straight to panic. Had she had breath or pulse, she might have considered it breath-taking or heart-stopping. Instead, she just found it terrifying.

And then she was in the grip of the angered waters of the lake, no longer cradled in the dubious safety of the *Mayflower* and subject to the whims of the running water.

There wasn't much that terrified a vampire, but this did.

She felt the thumps of people grabbing the casket in a desperate bid for safety. She heard the muted voices, but she couldn't respond.

She was too busy vomiting all over herself. She tried to pound her fists against the sides of her prison, but the pitching water stole all her strength. Ileen pressed ineffectual palms against the lid, trying to push it open, but she was as weak as a child. The nails held fast.

And what would you do if you did manage to pry the lid open?

Then came the awful, twisting horror, which made her try and curl into a ball, hampered only by the limited space of her casket. Instead, she lay, straining and trembling, on her side, her head and knees pushed tight to the wood, her palms tight to the side, desperate to feel the warmth and life of a living soul, as she vomited into the black soil that made her bed.

It lasted so long, she was sure she was dying. She had been convinced she would spend eternity in this damnable box, lying in her own filth.

Until it finally, blessedly stopped.

She laid her head back in the soil, brought her hands under her breasts, knitting her fingers together. She took long minutes to allow the last of the terror to slough away. When she finally believed she was in control of her mind again, she swallowed her gorge, tried to relax, and reached out to Chloe.

Assuming she's even still around. For all Ileen knew, the stupid child could be at the bottom of the lake, her lungs full of water and aquatic waste.

Well, that won't be me.

Ileen couldn't manage the mental peace required to cast out for her charge, so it came as an unpleasant surprise that the whelp had actually worked up the strength to cast out to *her*. She held her surprise in a vicious mental fist, not letting the whelp get a whiff of her shock.

First, Chloe said. *You live.*

Of course I do, whelp.

We passed the boundary.

Ah, so that's what had been twisting her in knots. She wasn't going to give Glory any hint of her suffering. Instead, she just sent, *What's happening?*

Chloe sent her images and snippets of sound and feeling, running them together until Ileen understood the alarming predicament they were in. And yet, for all of that, they were only minutes from the safety of the frozen shore.

Give me your eyes, Ileen demanded.

The whelp, to her credit, did so immediately, and Ileen looked around, seeing the rough wood of her prison, the incessant waves of water, the unceasing snow rifling in at an oblique angle to add to the thick layer of slush riding over the surface, the wind that first tossed water over Chloe's face and arms then immediately froze them.

She commanded Chloe to shake the frost clear, and she heaved her body up on the rocking casket — the motion forcing vomit from her throat once again and threatening to break the gossamer connection between First and charge — and squinted.

But she saw it. Not even a hundred yards away.

The shoreline.

Cruel, ice-slick rocks took all the punishment the lake could throw at them, and stood resolute. Beyond them, pine and birch trees twisted and bent and bore the weight of the ice on their limbs, bowed but not broken.

As she would have to be. Unbroken by this onslaught.

And, as Chloe had intimated, she knew this storm was not completely natural. Oh, it may have started that way, but she knew without a doubt that the elements had been whipped into a supernatural fury by a malevolent source.

The dogs.

Without a doubt.

Despite their current advantage, Ileen was going to get to that rock-strewn shore. She was going to escape this casket. She was going to do what needed to be done to get to that meeting place. She would prostrate herself before the dogs as necessary to negotiate the deal she needed.

And then she would make those fucking animals pay for this.

Without a doubt.

CHAPTER SIXTEEN

CHLOE'S SIGHT CAME back to her like the rising of the full moon, initially all in darkness, then faint details slowly resolving.

Through the entire time her Clutch leader had her senses, Chloe had fought to keep all images of Rory and Bertram out of her forethoughts. She knew that telling herself to not think about Rory only made her think of him more, so instead, she allowed herself to succumb, if only for a few teeth-grinding moments, to the wind and snow and, of course, the stomach-clenching, mind-numbing effect of simply being a vampire in running water.

It did the trick.

Now that the First was back in her own head, and Chloe was alone in her own, the first thing she did was check on the boy.

She didn't like what she saw.

He was no longer shivering.

He still had a pulse, though it was the merest whisper, barely pushing the fluid through his body. His breath was shallow, and the air coming out held no hint of warmth. She attempted to rouse him, and he was unresponsive. It was only because Kent had a grip on the boy's leg and she on his shoulder that he hadn't slipped off the tumbling casket.

She had to get him to shore.

Now.

"Kent! Zeke! Push! Kick with everything you have. REACH THE SHORE."

She didn't want to coerce the men, but she had no choice. She crunched her fingers through the rapidly thickening ice to get a better grip on Rory, then she forced her legs to kick at the damnable water.

She was so tired.

But she kicked.

The men were exhausted. They were suffering from extreme hypothermia themselves, the heat leached straight out of their bodies.

But still, they kicked.

They couldn't do otherwise.

Kent's face was a grim mask of focus and concentration.

Zeke simply screamed. Eyes clamped shut, fingers holding on only because they were frozen to the wood, jaw cracked wide, he screamed in agony.

The screaming went on far longer than it should have.

And then the casket hit something. Something hard and rough.

Chloe stopped kicking and allowed her feet to sink. They touched bottom.

The shore.

They'd made it to shore.

PART THREE
MEETING

"I have been so long master that I would be master still, or at least that none other should be master of me."

DRACULA
BRAM STOKER

CHAPTER SEVENTEEN

CHLOE WAS THE first ashore, dragging the limp body of Rory along with her. When she'd got him far enough from the crashing waves, she laid him gently up against a tree. It felt like positioning a rag doll.

She spared one more moment to just look at the boy's prone form. Then she went back for Kent and Zeke.

Zeke had managed to drag his friend half out of the water, but then his body failed him. She came up on the man and he looked at her, pain and exhaustion wracking his face. "I can't—" His voice broke with a sob. He gulped a frozen breath down and tried again. "I can't get him any higher up the shore," he said.

"I've got him," Chloe said. She planted her feet on the treacherous base of rock and snow, grabbed Kent by the sodden shoulders of his coat, and heaved. His head dropped back, exposing his white throat as his body lifted out of the water, but she only gritted her teeth and kept walking backward until she had him stretched on the ground beside Rory. Then she went back for Zeke.

He'd managed to remain sitting, but only barely. "Can you stand?"

"How?" he said, and she didn't understand the question.

"Come on, Zeke, help me."

"How can you still be going?" he said.

How indeed? Because I'm not in the water anymore. Because I'm not under the containment anymore.

Because I'm not human anymore.

"Because you need me to," she said.

"I don't think I can stand."

"Then do what you can and I'll help you."

Zeke leaned over, then rolled sloppily to hands and knees.

No time for subtlety, she thought, and grabbed him by the seat of his pants and collar and heaved him up the shore. She laid him gently beside Rory and Kent.

"We need to get a fire going."

"In a moment," Chloe said. "I have to get the casket."

"What?" Zeke said. "Why?"

She ignored him and trudged back through the path she had worn to the casket.

It was gone.

"Hell and damnation!"

No, not gone, just shifted several yards down the shoreline by the waves trying to spirit it away.

Chloe felt a momentary flash of desire to simply let it go. But no, they were here to broker a deal that would benefit their entire Clutch, to grant them freedoms they hadn't enjoyed since before Chloe was born.

The First was needed.

So Chloe stepped back into roiling, heaving, life-sucking Lake Kwanashishing to save her Clutch leader.

The waves immediately tried to pull her legs out from under her, but she leaned into the them, not fighting and let them lift and carry her closer to the pine box bobbing in the distance.

Minutes were frozen and slid by like hours until she could put her hands on the casket. She sent a brief message to her First. *Hold on, I'm getting you to land.* What came rocketing back into her head, strong enough for her to lose her grip momentarily, was *GET ME THE FUCK OUT OF HERE.*

It wasn't Voice, it was anger and indignation.

She thought, but only to herself, *I'm doing everything I can. DO.*

MORE.

Chloe closed down all thoughts and bent to the task of heaving the box up to shore, then hooking her fingers under the sodden, ice-crusted lid and dragging the wood against the resistance of the nails. Once she'd gotten some progress, some separation of lid from box, Ileen added her own meagre strength to it and, with the effort of both vampires, the lid was torn back and tossed to the ground.

The First pulled herself from her prison. Chloe had to use every shred of will and control to not react to the sight of her.

The thing that came out of the box was a nightmare. Her hair was wild, exploding from her head with thick dreadlocks of ice. From chin to the top of her breasts, she was covered in black, frozen vomit. It covered her arms and clawed, beringed fingers like some profane opera gloves. Her clothing—and she had chosen her most regal white gown for this meeting with the dogs—was equally black with regurgitated blood, and dark with the mud from the soil in the casket.

She looked for all the world like a cheap, lumber town harlot after a night of rough liquor and rougher sex. But Chloe kept that firmly to herself.

Instead of reacting, she held out a hand to help her First from the box, then led the way back through the snow-crusted forest to the three survivors.

Chapter Eighteen

CHLOE AND HER First entered the clearing just as Zeke started yelling for her.

"Glory! Help!"

He lay sprawled across Rory, frantically pulling on his tongue. "He's not breathing."

Chloe abandoned her First, not even thinking to gain her permission first, and ran to the child.

"I tried flipping him front to back like you're supposed to, but I didn't have the strength," he said. "I'm sorry, it's the only other thing I could think to do."

Chloe had heard of the tongue-pulling method to induce respiration, but had paid little attention to it.

She didn't hesitate. There was only one way to save this boy.

She hauled on her sleeve—the opposite to the one she'd used with Bertram—and tore into her arm with her teeth. The blood rose slowly, reluctant in the cold, but it rose.

She stood over Rory, a leg to either side of his body and, with her torn arm, she hauled him up to a standing position against the tree. With her free hand, she tilted his head back and yanked his mouth open. Then she grasped him by the jaw and held her torn arm over his mouth.

"You will not!"

Turning only her head, Chloe turned to her First. **"I will."**

"You *dare* to Voice me?"

Chloe turned back to the boy. *I'm going to die for this.*

But the First didn't stop her. Chloe sensed that, in Ileen's weakened state, while still able to throw off the Voice coercion, she could do little to stop her charge. Until she could, Chloe was going to keep Rory alive.

She let her blood drip into his mouth, could almost feel it slide down his cold throat, imagining the heat it trailed all the way down.

She hoped she wasn't too late, that he wasn't too far gone.

There were sounds behind her. Her First, moving through the snow. Likely coming to tear her head from her body.

So be it.

But the imagined attack never came.

Instead, she heard a short, low grunt, and then movement, first soft, then more energetic.

Once again, Chloe turned only her head, taking care to ensure she continued to feed Rory. Behind her, Kent was on his back in the snow, his pants pulled down to his knees. Ileen straddled him, sucking on the wound at his neck as she pushed herself up and down on his inevitable erection.

Ileen, not pausing in her pelvic thrusts, looked up at Chloe, her half-lidded eyes betraying her pleasure with both warm blood and stiffened cock, and said, "You have something to say, whelp?"

She did not. Instead, she twisted her head the other way to check on Zeke.

Who lay on the ground, his face a mask of horror.

"Who are you people?"

"Your…gods…" Ileen answered between thrusts. Then she moaned in ecstasy and orgasmed loudly.

"You're monsters," he said.

Yes, Chloe agreed, hearing the last of Ileen's gasps fall away, *we are.*

"**Sleep,**" she said.

Zeke's eyes closed.

Just as Rory's opened.

CHAPTER NINETEEN

RORY'S EYES OPENED, then they widened.

Chloe saw the reflexive movement of his throat as he took his first swallow of her blood, actually taking it into his body instead of letting it passively slide down his esophagus.

She watched as he mouthed "what...?" as his eyes flicked from her wrist to her face to Ileen still riding Kent's dead penis, back to her wrist, to Zeke, to the lake, to her wrist.

Then he reached up and pulled her arm down to his lips.

"Okay," Chloe whispered. "You've pulled enough from me." Zeke's eyes had closed, but there was still tenuous life inside him. "Feed off him." She pointed to Zeke.

She wanted to save Zeke as well as Kent, but she was pushing it just with Rory.

But Zeke and Kent saved us. She knew they'd never have made it to shore without the two of them pushing each other on through the cruelty of the water, the cold, the snow, and the wind.

Still, they could save them yet again.

Decent folk, she thought, then cast the thought to the winds.

"How?" Rory said, swiping a sleeve over his bloodied chin.

Chloe stared at him for a moment. He stared back, his eyes black pools. She sensed the question hanging there.

"You can speak."

He nodded. "Just…didn't want to with Father around," he said. "If he didn't like what I said, he'd make me pay." And Chloe heard it then, a blood memory. *You little sonofabitch, I'll make you pay.*

"I'll never do that to you," Chloe promised. She couldn't promise the same treatment from his new First.

He gave her another nod. "How do I—"

"Figure it out, fool," Ileen said, now finished with her profane copulation, standing and adjusting her skirts.

Rory moved to Zeke, crouched beside him. Chloe eased into his mind. *Push his head to one side. Expose the throat.*

Rory did.

Now, open him and feed.

Rory gave her a look, licked his lips, then blinked. He reached up with a finger, ran it along his teeth, stopping at the two much sharper and longer ones he found in his mouth. He touched them gingerly, his eyes seeking hers.

She gave him a nod.

"For fuck's sakes, child—" But he reacted before Ileen could finish her thought.

Chloe's Red King dropped his mouth to Zeke's throat and bit down, releasing a jet of blood. He drank feverishly, only at the beginning of his Eternal Hunger.

Chloe's own sang to her to join him, yet she held back, letting him take his fill.

It seemed to take forever.

Finally, the boy rose from Zeke's ruined neck. "It's…good."

She nodded. "You're still transitioning, Rory," she said. "I'm sure you feel much better, but you still need warmth. Open Kent up, put your hands inside him, deep as you can go, to warm them. We have nothing to start a fire."

"Yes, we do," he said.

Both Chloe and Ileen angled their heads in question.

Standing over Zeke, he pointed to him. "Zeke," he said. He bent, reached into an inside pocket of the man's coat, and pulled out a Mason jar sealed with paraffin. He waggled it. "Matches and some raw cotton to start a fire. He...told me? ...he'd read a story called *To Build a Fire* in London, and it scared him enough to always carry a watertight fire starter."

Chloe doubted Zeke had ever been to London. Either London. Ontario or England. Rory, still new to the thoughts of those they fed from flooding his brain, was probably messing up the author of that particularly grisly story.

Jack London.

She'd read it too.

As she recalled, the dog had fared better than the man. She hoped that wasn't a sign of how this night would go.

"Open up Kent," she said, taking the jar from him. "Warm yourself. I'll start the fire." *After I take the remainder of Zeke's blood and knowledge.*

She expected him to use his newfound teeth, but he surprised her by lifting Zeke, then reaching under him to pull a hunting knife from a sheath at his back.

She left him to his own devices and bent to her task. As she dragged the cooling blood from Zeke, thick, somewhat unpleasant, and mostly unsatisfying, she also dragged the last whispers from his mind, sorting through his store of knowledge and memories to tug at the right string to find...

Ah, there you are. And then she knew precisely what to do to get a fire going.

As she fed, it occurred to her that Zeke and Kent had saved them four times.

From the water.

With their blood.

With their warmth.

And now, with a fire.

There wasn't much left of Zeke, and she gave up trying to pull any more from him, her Hunger howling in protest. She ignored it as she usually did, instead standing and regarding the husk for one long moment.

You deserved a better end than this, she thought. *Both of you. I'm sorry you met me.*

Letting him go, she eyed Rory. He'd opened Kent from ribcage to genitals, and his hands were plunged elbow-deep in Kent's viscera. He had a look of bliss on his face, enraptured in the quality of warmth that could only be found inside a body.

You've shed your humanity quickly, Red King. I didn't expect it to happen so quickly, but vampire will always beat human.

Always.

"Chloe," the First said, and Chloe thought, *Yes, the fire.* She turned to the task at hand.

She passed Ileen, leaning against a tree in the lee of the wind and blowing snow. "Do we need to press on, My First?" she said.

"No, we're close enough that they'll come to us," she said, waving a hand casually. Ileen was very used to everyone coming to her. "Carry on and make your little fire for your whelp."

Chloe nodded.

"And Chloe?"

She stopped, looked back at her First over her shoulder.

"Don't get too attached to your pet. I did not ordain his making, and when we're done here, I will put him down."

Yet again, Chloe clenched down on all reaction, both physical and mental, only nodded and continued on her way.

But deep inside her, in the sullen, dark cave where she hid all her impure thoughts, she added one more to the ever-growing mound.

I'll kill you before I'll let you kill him.

Chapter Twenty

CHLOE GOT THE fire started, then got it roaring. She built it up, carefully brushing the snow off fallen wood, breaking long branches into smaller pieces bare-handed, and feeding them to the flames until they rose over her head.

There was no concern of anyone seeing the fire. They were miles from anywhere, the boat normally didn't make the trip this late, and the storm would keep any sane man inside.

She considered dropping Kent and Zeke's bodies into the flames to cover their feeding and the damage that had been visited upon them, but the forest's scavengers would likely cover their tracks even better.

She ignored the bodies and revelled in the warmth.

Rory joined her, standing at her side and holding his hands out, blood dripping from his elbows.

"Pull your clothes off, Rory," she said. "Clean yourself up."

"How?" he said. "With snow?"

She pointed to the flames.

"Like this, whelp," their First said, and Ileen strode past them, naked and filthy, snow clinging to her hair. She'd scrubbed at the worst of it with snow, and now she stepped carefully into the campfire.

Rory watched wide-eyed as the blood and dirt was burned away, as the snow in her hair melted, then the strands curled and burned and fell from her body in flaming clumps. Ileen stood, arms spread wide as though welcoming the flames.

Rory turned to Chloe, but continued to eye Ileen. "Does it hurt?"

"It does," Chloe said, "but only a little. It also feels very good."

They watched as the flames licked the Clutch First clean. She looked down, checking herself, then stepped back out of the fire, smiling. She stood in a patch of melting snow and brushed grey ash from her body. She looked older now, with the hair from her eyelashes, eyebrows, armpit, crotch, and head all burned away.

Yet, as she stepped over to her gown hanging from a branch, Chloe also had to admit she looked radiant, a phoenix from the flames.

Ileen regarded the gown. Despite her efforts, it remained blackened with vomit and stained with mud. With a disdainful toss, she discarded the garment in the fire. Soaked through, it landed hard and shifted the logs, sending sparks up to twist away in the wind, then hissed and steamed before finally catching fire.

Sensing motion, Chloe turned back to Rory, who was eagerly shrugging off his clothes, no sign of reluctance or embarrassment to be seen. He dropped the items wherever they left his body and, fully naked, ran into the fire.

Not a trace of hesitation, she thought as she watched him jump and land in the middle of the fire, the flames swirling higher than his head. He looked uncertain for only a moment, then a joyous smile creased his filthy face. *You're truly one of us.* She looked at the boy, surrounded and engulfed in flame.

My Red King.

Then he bent and stood again. Chloe couldn't help but giggle as the boy scrubbed the hot coals over his face and body like soap. He hadn't accepted what he was now. He was *embracing* it.

He emerged pink, hairless, and clean.

"That was fun!"

At the look of joy on his face, Chloe felt something she hadn't felt in a long time. She was seeing the world through his eyes.

She felt the wonder of being a vampire.

It was her turn for the fire, and she quickly stripped. She'd only gotten one step toward the heat, however, when she heard the crunch of snow, and Ileen.

"The dogs," Ileen said. "They've arrived."

Chapter Twenty-One

A HUGE WOLF stepped out of the trees and into the clearing, entering this dark, winter world from the shadows, the firelight reflecting back from its eyes. It gave a massive shake to shed the snow that had settled on its fur. Then the wolf warped with a sound that made Chloe want to retch.

The massive wolf was an equally massive human. The woman—Valda—was as naked as Rory and the First. Like them, she appeared unfazed by the storm of wind and snow swirling around her, though Chloe saw that it sharpened her nipples and whitened the hair at both head and crotch with sleet.

The woman smirked. "Pleasant trip, I presume?"

"How did you know where to find us?" Chloe asked, once again forgetting her place. It was the First's duty to greet the werewolves.

"Please," the woman said. "You don't need to be some German clerk in a patent office to figure this out." She stabbed a finger toward the bodies of Kent and Zeke. "We could smell dinner."

"They always waste the best parts." A naked man stepped up behind the pack leader, his height and bulk actually making Valda appear small. Despite him towering over her, his deference to her was obvious.

The woman's smirk widened into a full grin. "I must congratulate you on slipping your leash."

"No thanks to you, Valda," the First said.

"And what makes you say that, Ileen?" *They're feeling each other out, tossing each other's names around like they are nothing,* Chloe realized.

The First raised her arms. "This storm. It's unnatural. Supernatural."

Instead of rising to the bait, Valda tapped at her own head, saying, "I like what you've done with your hair." Then she smiled. Wider.

It was only with the increased display of teeth that Chloe remembered it was never good when a werewolf smiled. It was a challenge. Rory had eased himself back until he stood beside Chloe. She felt his hand find hers. *You're right to be scared, kid.*

Her First had to be seething. Yet, she held it together. Standing tall, the First met the pack leader's gaze and said, "I think we've danced enough, Valda. Neither of us truly wants to be here. Let's just get this done." She paused, waiting for Valda to say something, but the woman only crossed her arms over her naked breasts, inviting the First to continue. "Remove the boundary for my Clutch."

"It's not often that the dog has the opportunity to remove someone else's leash," Valda said. "Let me savour this moment, will you?"

"Valda..."

Chloe had only enough time to think, *Oh no...*

Chapter Twenty-Two

THE CHANGE WAS immediate. At the first hint of Voice, both Valda and her second dropped to all fours, hair, teeth, and claws sprouting, bodies bending and warping, but not fully morphing. The threat, however, was implicit. "You will not use your coercion tricks on me, bitch," Valda barked, saliva spraying. Her second only growled, fangs bared.

Her First reacted just as quickly. Her shoulders slumped as she dropped her head. "I apologize." Valda looked ready to spring. The First held out her hands. "Please. Accept my apology. You, of all people, must know that sometimes instinct takes over before the rational mind can step in and warn it off. I meant no disrespect."

Both Valda and her second visibly relaxed, fur and claws and teeth slipping back into more human forms, the fire banked, if not extinguished.

Chloe stood by, stunned by what she had just witnessed. It had been insincere, of course. But still. She had never seen her First prostrate herself—basically offer her belly—to anyone in all the time she'd known her. But she had. And willingly.

Did Ileen truly not think three vampires—even if one was only minutes old—could best two lowly werewolves?

No, Chloe, remember, this is not about beating the wolves. This is about negotiating with them. I must try and remember that.

The two werewolves stood once again.

"Can we start over?" the First said, and got a nod in return. "Good." She paused a moment, then nodded as well. "I'd like to talk about you removing the boundary for us."

"Better, Ileen," Valda said. "Better." She turned to her second, and gave him a nod. He immediately slipped back into the darkness between the trees. She turned back to the First. "To be clear, in return for abolishing the boundary and letting your Clutch loose on the world, you're offering…?"

"In return, I can offer to abolish all servitude of your race to mine. This will include all in my Clutch, now and in future, and any Clutch affiliated with mine. Even if I pass, the agreement would live on."

"Very good. There's still some nitty-gritty details to work out, to eliminate any loopholes." Valda smiled, looked around. "Because we're quite aware of how a vampire can exploit loopholes, aren't we?"

Before the First could respond, Valda's second loped back out of the forest, an ornate staff held in its mouth. Even in the darkness, Chloe saw the sharpened base, the ornate carving of a cat at the head, and runes running its length.

As he lifted his head to offer the staff to Valda, Chloe noticed the snow seemed to bend around it, never contacting.

She was twenty feet away, yet still, she felt its power thrumming in the darkness. *The Staff of Solomon.*

Valda reached out with both hands and gently took the Staff from her second. Then she turned back to the First and lifted the Staff above her head.

Instantly, the wind ceased, the snow fell straight down, then also ceased, and the cold lessened considerably.

The storm that had caused them so much trouble, that had sunk the *Mayflower*, was gone almost instantly.

Looking around her at the sudden calm, Valda said, "That's a little better, isn't it?"

It was *you who made the storm.* Chloe kept her treacherous mouth shut, and squeezed Rory's hand hard enough to warn him to do the same.

"Thank you," the First said, politely. "Now, if you could do the same for the bound —"

"Not until the blood oath is completed, Ileen."

"And how can I be sure you'll pull the boundary afterward?"

"It's a blood oath, Ileen," Valda said. "How can I be sure you'll release us all from vampire slavery? We're only as good as our word, *First*." That last said with a thick sarcasm.

"You are correct, pack leader, our word holds tremendous weight, as our names do. However, I would also say I have ample reason to doubt your word after the storm you sent."

"I didn't send it, vampire," Valda hissed between clenched teeth. "I merely enhanced it."

"Pull the boundary," the First said.

As her second shifted fully back to human form, Valda lifted the Staff once again above her head, as though she was going to do just that.

Then she twisted the Staff and drove the pointed tip forcefully into the snow and sand between her feet.

"I think you misunderstand," Valda said. "This is a *meeting.* This is a *negotiation.* This is *not* one side demanding the other do as they're told. Being told what *has* to be done. As blood drinkers have always done with the wolves. Demand this, and command that. And still, you keep telling me I must fulfill my part of the agreement first only because I'm in the position of power. Because I hold all the cards." She ran a hand up and down the runed surface of the Staff, seemingly mesmerized by it. "Or, in this case, I hold both the Book and the Staff of Solomon."

"It was sheer luck that either fell into your hands, Valda," the First said. "We both know that."

"Oh, Ileen," Valda said, eyes dancing in the firelight, "you are so unsuited to jealousy. The Book came along at the right time, and allowed us to restrict your movements."

"The Book seems to gravitate to the under*dog*." She leaned hard on that last syllable.

"The why doesn't matter. The fact of the matter is, the boundary was set up in perpetuity with the Book." She studied the Staff in her hand once again, stroking sensually with her eyes. "And only this—the fabled Staff of Solomon—can bend that absolute and set you free."

"All things we're aware of."

"But you keep forgetting an important part of the equation, Ileen." Her eyes kept stroking the rune-covered Staff.

"And that is…?"

"That it's only going to happen if I decide to allow it. And before that can happen…" Valda tore her eyes away and eyed the First. "…you need to learn your place."

CHAPTER TWENTY-THREE

"Y OU SOUND LIKE my dad."

Rory, Chloe sent. *Hush.*

The First directed a withering glare first at Rory for his outburst, then at Chloe, presumably for making him in the first place.

Valda looked down at the boy, as though seeing him for the first time. "Another county heard from," she said, her tone biting. "You have something to say, infant?"

"Rory," Chloe said. **"Hush."**

Rory ignored both Chloe's admonishment and his First's glare. Chloe thought, *How…?*

Instead, he took several steps forward, stared at the monstrous woman and even more monstrous man in front of him and, exhibiting no fear, said again, "You sound like my dad."

Valda chuckled low, in the back of her throat. It was not a pleasant sound.

"I didn't mean it as a compliment," Rory said.

At another glare from her First, Chloe moved forward to grab the boy, but Valda raised a hand. "Leave him be, blood drinker. I want to hear what he says. I find him refreshingly entertaining."

Chloe stopped, frozen between obeying her First and not offending the pack leader who literally held their freedom in her hand.

Valda took a knee, leaning on the Staff for support. Her eyes and teeth gleamed in the firelight as she motioned with her free hand at Rory. "Carry on, boy. Say your piece."

Rory... Chloe sent, thickening it with as much warning as she could relay.

He ignored her.

"My dad used to say that to my mom," Rory said.

Valda angled her head in question.

"'You need to learn your place, woman,' he'd say." Chloe watched his small hands clench into fists. "Then he'd hit her. He hit her a lot."

"A sad tale, to be sure, but—"

"When she died, he did it to me. Said that to me. Hit me. Did...other stuff."

"And where is this nefarious father now? Should this be part of the negotiation, to kill this man?"

"No, Valda—" the First started, but the pack leader raised a silencing hand.

"He has the floor, Ileen," Valda said, barely granting the First a glance. "He's obviously got something to say, let the boy speak. 'Out of the mouth of babes hast thou ordained strength' and all that." She turned back to Rory. "You were saying..."

"You don't have to kill my father," Rory said. "Chloe already did that for me."

"Did she now?"

"She saved me." He held up two fingers. "Twice."

"A spellbinding story, I'm sure," Valda said, then growled, "get to the point, boy."

"My dad was a bad man," Rory said.

And Chloe thought, *Oh no...*

"And he did bad things to my mom and me," Rory said.

And Chloe thought, *No...*

"And he died," Rory said.

And Chloe took a step forward...

"You sound like him," Rory said.

A second step.

"And you want to do bad things to us," Rory said.

Another step.

"So you should die," Rory said. He pounced, jumping, clearing twenty feet from a standing start, and landed on Valda, teeth flashing as he sought to rend her flesh from her bones.

Chapter Twenty-Four

Rory leapt.

"**Rory! No!**" Chloe couldn't keep the Voice at bay, useless as it was against him. As she surged forward, she thought, *Godsdamnit!*

In the span of that thought, Rory seemed to be everywhere, a rapacious spider darting in to bite or slash, then pull back, only to slip in from another angle.

A thought from Ileen stabbed into her brain in the shred of time it took for Chloe to leave the ground and thrust herself forward at the two figures, vampire and werewolf, Rory and Valda, and that thought was *we need that Staff.*

Valda was screaming. Rory had lasted far longer than Chloe would have expected. Likely only because he was so damned small and Valda was so large. She watched as the pack leader made a grab for him, but her hand came down on cold air. He'd squirted out and pressed his attack elsewhere. He attacked with no skill, no method, just grappling for the closest part, clenching arms or legs or both around a limb, a joint, and darting in with teeth flashing to tear and rend, then skip away before he could be trapped again.

The pack leader was bleeding from multiple places, and with her concentration split between grabbing at the child and defending herself, couldn't seem to focus on transitioning to wolf.

Her second stood behind her, at the ready. He would not interfere unless Valda called him in to help, but he stood low to the ground, hands outstretched.

Chloe's feet touched the ground, Ileen's thought stuck in her mind like a dagger to the skull. Valda saw her come, saw her reach out for the Staff, and the pack leader forgot about Rory for a moment, slashed up with the Staff, and lightning shot across Chloe's cheek and her feet left the ground once more as she sailed first up, then crashed back to the frozen earth and snow, coming to rest against the corpse of Kent. It took her a moment to push herself back up, one palm tight against her face.

The spinning in her head slowed and she was able to get her bearings. She was thirty feet back from the two of them, on the far side of the campfire, and from the feel of it, her face flayed open from the corner of her eyebrow down her cheek to her jawline. The skin had been stripped back and she felt bone and ligaments.

"Bitch," she said, and stood again.

The First was closer to the two scrambling figures. She moved in from the side, angling for the Staff, but again, despite Rory's mosquito attacks, Valda saw it coming. She barked something and heaved the Staff behind her. Her second had been ready and caught it, just as Ileen moved in.

Without a second's hesitation, without mercy, almost without thought, the large man brought the Staff back over his shoulder, both hands holding it well back.

Then he drove the ornately carved wooden Staff forward and straight through the First's chest, the sharp tip easily punching through her breast, and out through her back again.

Ileen let out a wailing sound like Chloe had never heard before, and it was like the pain was too big to be held in only the First's head because it roiled out of her, invisible waves of agony, and punched into Chloe's head, dropping her to her knees.

And then the big man pulled the Staff out savagely, shifted his grip, then swung It around even as Ileen was falling. The cat's-head carving at the other end hit her squarely on the side of the head, just under the ear.

The blow tore her head off.

The agony instantly ceased in Chloe's mind, and the silence roared at her.

The First is dead. Kill the wolf.

Chapter Twenty-Five

EVERYTHING SEEMED TO speed up, multiple actions happening at once, overlapping each other.

Chloe stepped to one side of the fire.

Valda stood and barked something unintelligible to her second.

Her second turned and ran back into the shadow of the forest, Staff in hand.

"No!" Chloe's shout went out, then disappeared like smoke from the fire.

Valda dropped to all fours and, with a loud wrench, she turned her savaged form from woman to wolf. Where there had been flesh and hands and teeth there was now fur and claws and fangs. It took no longer than a single, violent second. Her tail was still growing out as she sprang and landed over Rory.

She's going to kill him.

Chloe rarely used the unnatural speed vampires possessed. It was only good over short distances, but it drained the reserves quickly. And Chloe had spent hours on that gut-twisting running water and, even worse, more hours in it. She hadn't fed well, had, in fact, given up some of herself just to get Bertram to survive.

She was drained. Weak.

But she had rage on her side.

And she had that unnatural speed.

Even as Valda's head began its downward plunge toward Rory, Chloe surged, her movements blurring faster than eyes could track, one hand dipping to grab her weapon. One moment, she was by the campfire, then, in a fraction of a heartbeat, she was in front of Valda, a shard of burning wood glowing white-hot from its swift passage. Chloe raised it as Valda's jaws begin to encircle Rory's tiny neck.

Then, even as the sparks from the campfire were only now beginning to rise from the disturbed base, Chloe wrapped her fingers tight around the burning shard and thrust it forward with all the supernatural speed her blood-enhanced muscles could offer, and stabbed the point into Valda's left eye.

Valda screamed, her jaws reflexively closing, but Chloe was faster—though slowing now—and she yanked Rory viciously out from between her jaws and threw him behind her.

Valda screamed a full-throated roar of pain as she swiped claws at her mostly unseen attacker.

With her last surge of speed, Chloe easily evaded the slow-motion attack, and reached out and plucked the shard from Valda's face. She had to tug at it, as the flesh had burned and melded to the wood. It took some effort, but she got it out.

Then she stabbed it into Valda's other eye, completely blinding her.

Chloe was exhausted, and wanted to rest, but even as Valda's screams escalated, the vampire knew she could still be found. That damnable wolf sense of smell.

She had no more surging left in her, and reality spiralled back up to its normal pace.

Chloe took a step back, and took two deep breaths.

Valda was still in pain. But given enough time, Chloe knew she would heal.

Wolves always healed.

That couldn't happen. Not today. Not with Valda.

Chloe lunged forward, one hand catching Valda's thin, tapered chin, and she pushed the wolf's head up toward the sky. Then she leaned in and tore Valda's throat out.

Just like you were going to do with Rory, you bitch.

Valda slumped and Chloe let her go, watching her form drop to the snow.

Chloe, more out of sheer survival instinct than anything, bent and fed from the wolf. Wolf blood was not the best, but, like any animal, it would do if there were no humans about.

When her thirst was mostly slaked, she knew she had one more thing to do, and she had to do it quickly. Valda's pack wouldn't stay gone for long.

Glancing over at Rory, who was sitting up and watching her, she turned back to the wolf, gripped her at the base of her neck and by the jaw. Then, muscles bunching and heaving, Chloe tore her head off.

EPILOGUE

"WHERE ARE WE going?"

Chloe kept walking, but said, "Back to the boundary." Thinking, *I must be insane. Rory and I are free. We could go anywhere.*

They could. But they would be hunted mercilessly. She'd killed a pack leader. Never mind that they had killed her Clutch leader first.

"We gonna be able to get through it?"

"I think so. It was created to keep us in, not to keep things out."

"Okay," he said. Then, moments later, "Did you really need to bring those?" He pointed at the objects she carried in each hand.

"I did," she said. "You'll see why when we get back."

That seemed to appease him. They fell into a companionable silence.

The boundary hadn't been far from where the disastrous meeting had occurred. Forty-five minutes after they had left the clearing, Chloe began recognizing some of the landmarks. And there was a tingling in her scalp.

And there were about twenty Clutch members standing just a few yards away, on the other side of the boundary.

She stopped. Turned to Rory. "We're going to cross the boundary in a minute," she said. "It's probably going to hurt some."

"I can take it."

Spoken with the brashness of the uninformed, she thought, but gave him a smile. "Then let's go home."

She was right. It did hurt.

But not as much as when she went through the first time.

When they staggered into the middle of the Clutch, their members caught them, supported them.

It took surprisingly little time to tell them all about what had occurred. Then she held up the first of the two objects in her hand.

"The First was killed," she said simply. The Clutch members stared at Ileen's severed head.

"And though I could not get to the one who killed her, I took their pack leader," she said, holding up the second head. "Their First."

She let both arms drop, but didn't let go of the heads.

"I could have taken the boy and been free of the boundary," she said. "But I didn't. I couldn't."

"Why not?" a Clutch member said. "No one would have held it against you." There were nods of assent.

"It's no secret that the First and I rarely saw eye to eye," she said. "I will admit to never having accepted her as First." She paused then, her eyes turning back to the water. She stared at it for a long moment.

"I could not respect a leader who showed little respect for those she led." Nods of assent yet again, but more tentative this time. Wary.

"I do respect the Clutch members. I would be your First, if you would have me."

"You and the First went to broker our freedom," another member stated. "We're still not free, the First is gone, and the dogs still possess both Book and Staff."

Chloe nodded.

"Still, you brought us a fighter, and you took their leader," said a third. They looked to the other members. "We will talk on it," the member said, and that was all Chloe could ask for.

"Sunrise will come soon. We should head back to safety."

"I'll be right behind you," Chloe said. As they turned for home, she stepped wearily down to the shoreline, and stood, gazing out at the waters of Lake Kwanashishing.

"What are you doing, Chloe?"

I've got to teach you the consequences of tossing around names like you do, she thought.

"Just thinking about standing here a few months back," she said. "I had an idea, but I guess it was stupid."

She swung her arm back and heaved Valda's head out into the water. It flew in a high arc before coming down in a titanic splash.

Then, choosing a different location, she did the same with Ileen's head. Once again, she tracked it as it arced upward, still travelling outward, past the boundary, then down and into the water.

"I thought it was a good idea," she said. "But it got a lot of people killed, and probably destroyed any chance of us ever getting away from here."

Rory stood beside her, watched the ripples fade back into the small waves that coasted along the surface.

"Yes," he said. "But still, you and her did get free. You chose to come back." Then he pointed out to the lake. "And in the end, she's free of the boundary forever." He touched her shoulder. "That's something, isn't it?"

"I guess it is," Chloe said. "I guess it is." She brought a hand up, touched Rory's still on her shoulder.

"Let's go home, Red King."

◆ ◆ ◆

1953

Forty years ago. A blink of the eye for a vampire. But in forty years, she and Rory, Red, the Red King, had become brother and sister. Shed blood, spilled blood, and shared blood.

One final glance at Red, then Chloe — *Glory. You're Glory right now* — turned and knocked on the door to Will's house.

Let's see if we can find another brother, she thought.

Author's Note

THIS ONE WAS a weird one, start to finish.

I think I've previously mentioned that my fictional town of New Hope is based on the real town of Barry's Bay, Ontario, a place I lived in for four short, but very influential and formative years. With the additional stories I wrote that took place in the area, I eventually included Carry's Cove (yes, it sounds like a bad pseudonym for Barry's Bay, but it's really the neighbouring town of Combermere to the south), and the vampire town of Vilni that, showing virtually no imagination on my part, is really the town of Wilno, just with the letters mixed up a bit.

I should mention that Wilno has (or at least had, in the late 1970s) the weird reputation of being the Vampire Capital of Canada. I kid you not. In fact, while I lived there, apparently a certain rag of a newspaper written for those with so-called *Enquiring Minds* even sent some reporters up to write an article.

Anyway, what has all this to do with this strange little historical story?

Well, there was a point where I reconnected with an old high school friend from the area, and she happened to mention one day the boating disaster that happened on Lake Kamaniskeg between Barry's Bay and Combermere. And apparently, some people had survived the frigid November waters by floating to safety clutching a casket. This had happened November 12, 1912, only seven months after the Titanic.

I'd lived there for four years. We literally had a house with lake frontage. I swam in that lake virtually every day between May and September. And I had never ever heard about this.

This was one hell of a story. How the hell had I missed it?

My friend was also shocked. "After all," she said, "they even had the story on the paper placemats in the Wilno Tavern."

And, somehow, it had never entered my consciousness.

Anyway, I had already planned to add vampires to my little universe (see the upcoming *Blood Relations*), but when I heard about this, I knew I had to do something with it. And the little fact that its story had, at least at one time, been printed on placemats in a tavern in the Vampire Capital of Canada, well, it seemed logical that it had to somehow incorporate vampires as well.

But how?

For quite a few years, the answer was "damned if I know!"

Well, flash forward to the crazy COVID times of 2020 and 2021. In those lazy, hazy, crazy days of lockdown, I managed to get a fair amount of writing done, including the long-gestating vampire novel, *Blood Relations*. When I finished it, I knew what my next project was going to be.

I just…didn't know what the actual story was…

But, with little else to do but sit around and throw ideas against the wall like half-cooked spaghetti noodles, I came up with a combo deal of a couple of different takes. One would have involved a single vampire on the voyage, and ending up with the coffin sinking into the lake. I loved the idea…but I didn't know how to get that damn vampire back up and out of the lake.

The other one was to have two vampires, but one of them was going to have silver teeth implanted, all the better to kill you with, my dear wolf. I kind of angled toward that one.

I'd also written about my vampires, Chloe and Rory, in *Blood Relations*, and I knew that this story would ultimately sit just before that one, so why not introduce the two in this story and give them both a bit of a backstory?

I jotted down my story beats and started to write.

And, as per usual, Chloe and Rory and Ileen and Valda all started yelling at me from the side of stage, telling me my ideas were shit, and they had better ones.

So, I listened to them. I think they were right. Their ideas were better than my shit.

What do you think?

About the Author

TOBIN ELLIOTT HAS written for most of his life. After some unfortunate incidents with walls and permanent markers, he switched to safer things like pens and paper, and later, typewriters and then computers. Though science fiction was his first love, horror has always had a powerful hold on him, even back before he wore big-boy pants. He likes to have the shit scared out of him, and he likes scaring the shit out of others. Somehow, it always comes down to shit with Tobin.

Tobin spent his formative teenage years in a small town about four hours northeast of Toronto. Those experiences, and the magic and wonder of that place, never left him, though he left the town through no fault of his own. He currently lives within a three-hour drive of the place, and occasionally gets back to top up on his sense of wonder and nostalgia.

Based on that town and surrounding areas, Tobin has written several novels in his Aphotic World series.

Along with those writings, Tobin has been fortunate enough to have had three horror novellas published, as well as seven stories in various anthologies. He has been a board member of both the Writers' Community of Simcoe County (WCSC) and the Writers' Community of Durham Region (WCDR), and, for five years, was an annual participant in the Muskoka Novel Marathon, a 72-hour writing marathon to raise money for adult literacy programs.

Finally, he also taught creative writing for two different continuous learning programs. Tobin writes ugly stories about bad people doing horrible things, and it was his pleasure to show other people how to do the same thing for almost twenty years.

If you're interested in more ramblings by Tobin, well, he's not much into social media. He sees it as a blight on humanity of almost Bookian proportions. And yet, still, he's on there.

Facebook: The Horror Guy (/tobinelliott.horrorguy)

Twitter: @TheHorrorGuy91

Instagram: @tobinelliott.horrorguy

♦ ♦ ♦

I HOPE THAT this book captured your imagination, and I hope that this series will turn you into a loyal reader.

Because loyal readers are an author's secret weapon. They can influence other readers…how?

Through reviews.

If you loved this book, and yes, even if you hated it, please also consider leaving a review on the site where you purchased it, and/or Goodreads, or anywhere else. You can also drop me a line at TheHorrorGuy91@gmail.com.

As a reader, you have an immense power to influence others.

Please, use that power.